This book belongs to

_____

Dora's READY-TO-READ Adventures

Based on the TV series *Dora the Explorer*® as seen on Nick Jr.®

SIMON SPOTLIGHT
An imprint of Simon & Schuster Children's Publishing Division
1230 Avenue of the Americas, New York, New York 10020
Dora's Picnic; Follow Those Feet!; and *Dora in the Deep Sea* © 2003
Viacom International Inc. *I Love My Papi!* and *Say "Cheese!"* © 2004
Viacom International Inc. All rights reserved.

2 4 6 8 10 9 7 5 3
ISBN 0-689-87815-X
These titles were previously published individually by Simon Spotlight.
These titles were previously catalogued individually by the Library of Congress.

Dora's READY-TO-READ Adventures

Ready-to-Read

Simon Spotlight/Nick Jr.

New York   London   Toronto   Sydney

Contents

Dora's Picnic

8

by Christine Ricci   illustrated by Susan Hall

Hi! I am . We are going to a picnic at Play Park! Play Park has a  SLIDE, a SANDBOX, and SWINGS.

My **mami** is helping me make  -and- PEANUT-BUTTER JELLY sandwiches for the picnic.

 is my best friend.
BOOTS

He loves **!**
BANANAS

 BOOTS **has a bunch of** **BANANAS**
for the picnic.

BENNY is riding his **BICYCLE** to the picnic.

14

He is carrying juice

APPLE

in his .

BASKET

Here comes the .

The has a big of

 for the picnic.

Yummy!

Look!  has a bowl of
BABY BLUE BIRD
fruit in her 🛒 .
WAGON

The fruit bowl has ,

, and .

BANANAS

APPLES

GRAPES

19

What did  bring to
the picnic?

TICO

 brought .

TICO   BREAD

The is filled with

       BREAD

and   !

BLUEBERRIES   NUTS

ISA made **CUPCAKES** to share with everyone.

I like chocolate  CUPCAKES

with PINK icing. What kind

do you like?

Look out for .

SWIPER

He will try to swipe the food we brought.

 is hiding behind

SWIPER

the .

TREE

Say, "Swiper, no swiping!"

Yay! You stopped !

SWIPER

We made it to Play Park! This  TABLE is perfect for our picnic. But first we want to play!

likes to go down

TICO

the .

SLIDE

27

is making a
BABY BLUE BIRD   SAND CASTLE

in the **.**
SANDBOX

The pushes

BIG RED CHICKEN **BOOTS**

and on the .

ISA **SWINGS**

29

This is the best picnic!
We can all share the food.
What would **you** bring
to a picnic?

Follow Those Feet!

by Christine Ricci   illustrated by Susan Hall

Hi! I am .
DORA
 and I found
BOOTS
some in the .
FOOTPRINTS **SANDBOX**
I wonder who made them.

Do you know?

Did I make these ?

FOOTPRINTS

No, my feet are small.

I did not make these .

FOOTPRINTS

Did  make these ?

BOOTS   **FOOTPRINTS**

No, his are shaped

FOOTPRINTS

like an oval. He did not

make these .

FOOTPRINTS

36

Who made these ?

FOOTPRINTS

We can follow them to find out.

Hello, !
BIG RED CHICKEN

Did you make these ?
FOOTPRINTS

No, his feet have three toes! He did not make these  .

FOOTPRINTS

Did the  make

HORSE

these ?

FOOTPRINTS

40

No, the horse wears  HORSESHOES on her feet. She did not make these FOOTPRINTS.

41

Did the  make these footprints?

No, the  has long

CROCODILE

nails. He did not make

these .

FOOTPRINTS

43

Did the  make the  ?

RABBIT   FOOTPRINTS

No, she has two long feet

and two short feet.

She did not make these

FOOTPRINTS

Did the 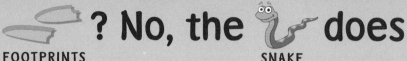 make these
SNAKE
? No, the  does
FOOTPRINTS   SNAKE
not have feet!

He slides across the ground. He did not make these  .

FOOTPRINTS

Do you see ? Did
SWIPER   SWIPER

make these ?
FOOTPRINTS

No,  is sneaky!
SWIPER
He tiptoes. He did not
make these .
FOOTPRINTS

49

The  go all the way to
FOOTPRINTS
the beach!

They go by the
SHELLS

toward the  .
SAND CASTLE

Now do you know who
made these  ?

FOOTPRINTS

It was  ! He walked to
BENNY

the beach in his new  !
FLIPPERS

Yay! We did it! We found
out who made the !

FOOTPRINTS

Dora in the Deep Sea

by Christine Ricci   illustrated by Robert Roper

Hi! I am . This is .

DORA   **BOOTS**

And here is our friend,

.  looks sad.

PIRATE PIG   **PIRATE PIG**

What is wrong, ?

PIRATE PIG

"I have lost my !"

TREASURE CHEST

says . "The

PIRATE PIG   TREASURE CHEST

fell off my and

SHIP

into the 🌊 !"

SEA

58

and I will help

BOOTS   **PIRATE PIG**

find his .

TREASURE CHEST

Will you help too?

We need something to take
us down into the .
SEA
What can take us into the
 ?
SEA

60

A can take us down
SUBMARINE
into the !
SEA

Ooh, we are going down into the  .

SEA

Look! A  !

SAND CASTLE

Hello, !

KING CRAB

63

There is a  FISH with SPOTS

by the ROCK .

64

I see a  . . . and a funny

STARFISH

clownfish!

Boots spots a 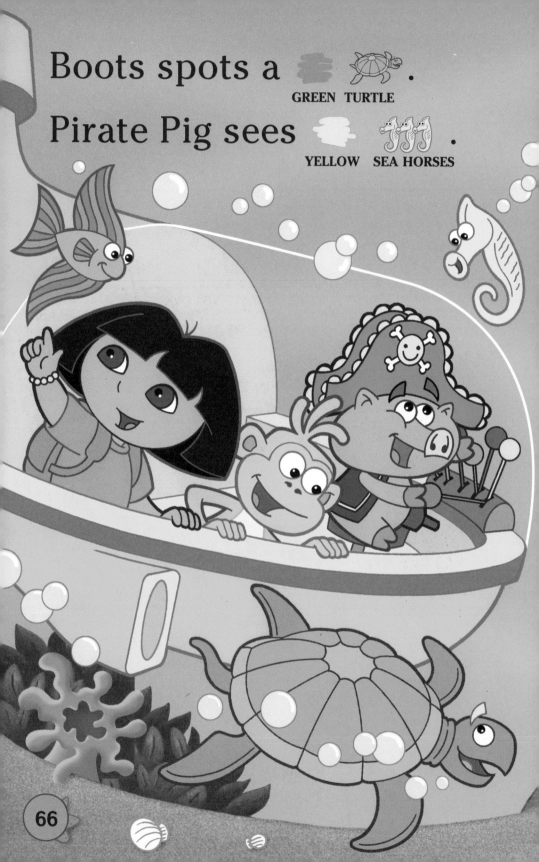 🐢 .

GREEN TURTLE

Pirate Pig sees 🦐🦐🦐 .

YELLOW SEA HORSES

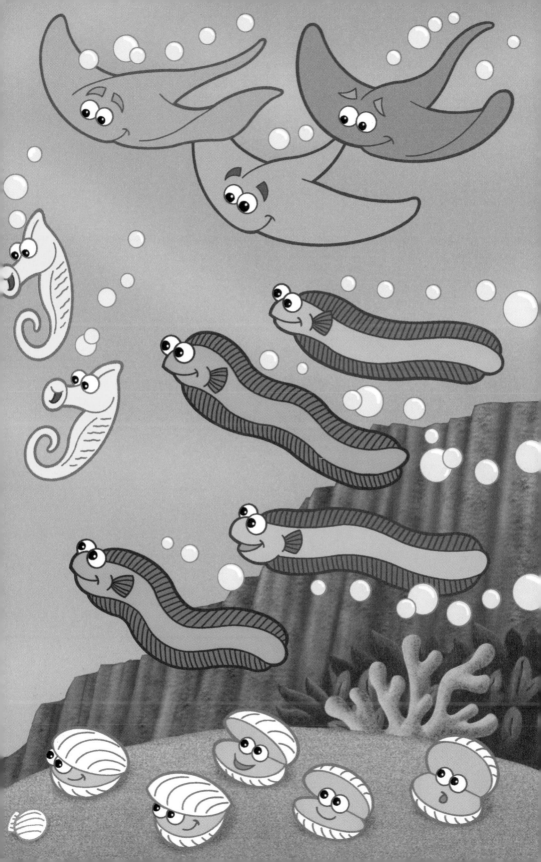

Oh, no! Here come some !

LOBSTERS

They will try to pinch

the  with their ⬤⬤!

SUBMARINE   CLAWS

We drove the 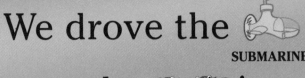 SUBMARINE

past the ![lobsters] ! LOBSTERS

Now we need to find

the ![treasure chest] . TREASURE CHEST

Hooray! We found the  !

TREASURE CHEST

72

But we have to watch out

for .

SWIPER

He will try to swipe

the .

TREASURE CHEST

Do you see ?

SWIPER

Look! is behind the !

SWIPER WHALE

He is going to swipe

the  !

TREASURE CHEST

We have to say " SWIPER , no swiping!"

You helped us stop !

Yay! has his 📦 !

PIRATE PIG   **TREASURE CHEST**

Thank you for helping!

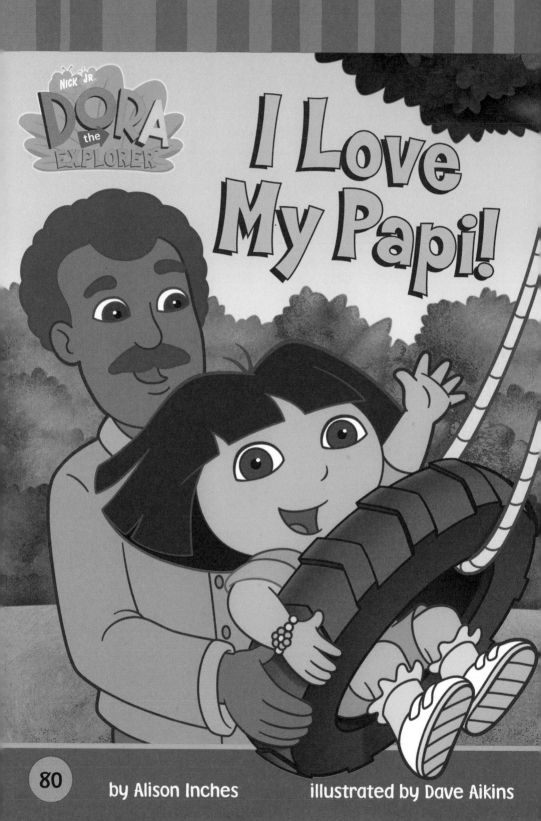

I Love My Papi!

by Alison Inches   illustrated by Dave Aikins

My  and I love to do things together!

PAPI

PAPI **taught me a super soccer kick. Look, I kicked the**  **SOCCER BALL** **into the**  **GOAL** **!**

We also love playing .
 coaches my team.

BASEBALL

PAPI

He taught us how to swing the  and slide into home .

BAT

BASE

On weekends  and I
PAPI
ride ![bikes] together.
BIKES

Or sail on a  .
BOAT

Sometimes we go to the 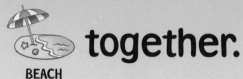 together.

BEACH

We build giant and
SAND CASTLES

play in the .
WAVES

My  is a really good .

PAPI **COOK**

He taught me how to bake

a special  and make

CAKE

yummy .

SANDWICHES

90

Sometimes we pack a  PICNIC

and share it with my

friend BOOTS.

93

My  made us this

PAPI

TIRE

swing! He can build

anything with .

TOOLS

94

One time  took us to
PAPI
the  .  loved the  .
CIRCUS   BOOTS   CLOWNS

96

Then bought us and

PAPI

POPCORN

 for a treat.

STRAWBERRY ICE CREAM

Yum! Yum!

At the end of every day  tucks me into .

PAPI

BED

100

Then we read a .

BOOK

I like  about .

BOOKS

ANIMALS

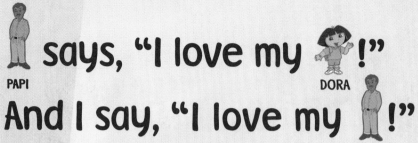 says, "I love my !"

And I say, "I love my !"

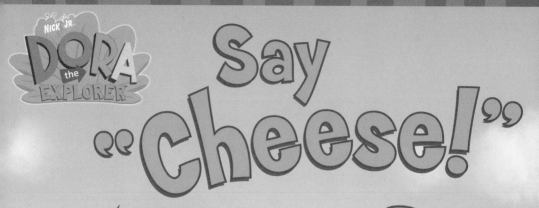

Say "Cheese!"

by Christine Ricci   illustrated by Steven Savitsky

Hi! I am
DORA
. My friend
BOOTS
is sick today.

How can we cheer him up?

105

I know! We can visit

BOOTS

at his .

TREE HOUSE

And we can use my

CAMERA

to take pictures of things

 likes.

BOOTS

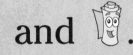 would love a picture

BOOTS

of and .

BACKPACK   MAP

Say "  !"

CHEESE

We are at Mountain.
STAR

 Mountain is filled
STAR

with .
STARS

 loves to play with
BOOTS

the !
STARS

Look! There is .
TOOL STAR

 has all kinds of .
TOOL STAR   TOOLS

Say " !"
CHEESE

Here is a fruit garden.

Which fruit does 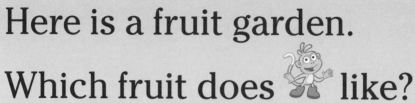 like?

Yes, BOOTS loves BANANAS!

Who else loves 🍌?
BANANAS

The 🐦!
BIRD

Say "🧀!"
CHEESE

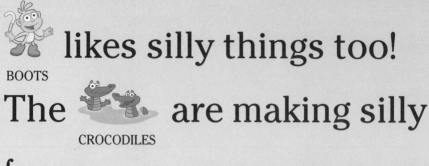 likes silly things too!

The  are making silly

faces.

Ha, ha, ha! Smile,  !

CROCODILES

Say "  !"

CHEESE

Do you see more

silly things?

113

has baked a

for .

Yummy!

made a for .

BENNY　　　　　　　CARD　　　BOOTS

 and look at

ISA　　　　　　BENNY

the .

CAMERA

Say "  !"

CHEESE

115

likes to swing

BOOTS

through the .

JUNGLE

 likes to swing

DIEGO

through the too!

JUNGLE

likes to play

BABY JAGUAR

in the

FLOWERS

Say "

CHEESE

!"

Here is an cart.
ICE-CREAM

 loves !
BOOTS   ICE CREAM

Say " !"
CHEESE

Uh-oh. Do you see someone behind the 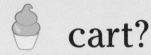 cart?

ICE-CREAM

It is  !

SWIPER

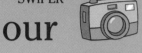 wants to swipe

SWIPER

our .

CAMERA

We have to stop .

SWIPER

Say " , no swiping!"

SWIPER

121

Yay! We stopped !

Hey, there is !

 will give us a ride
TICO

to the  in his .
TREE HOUSE   CAR

Say "  !"
CHEESE

Hooray! We made it to the .

And loves all the

pictures!

We cheered up .

BOOTS

Thanks for helping!

Oh, I have to take **1**
ONE
more picture.
 wants a picture of
BOOTS
you!
Say "  !"
CHEESE